Seamore,
the Very Forgetful Porpoise,

by Darcie Edgemon

illustrated by J. otto Seibold

HARPERCOLLINSPUBLISHERS

Seamore, the Very Forgetful Porpoise

Text copyright © 2008 by Darcie Edgemon

Illustrations copyright © 2008 by J.otto Seibold

Manufactured in China.

Library of Congress Cataloging-in-Publication Data is available.
ISBN-10: 0-06-08057-2 (trade bdg.) — ISBN-13: 978-0-06-085075-3 (trade bdg.)
ISBN-10: 0-06-085076-0 (lib. bdg.) — ISBN-13: 978-0-06-085076-0 (lib. bdg.)

Typography by Rachel L. Schoenberg
1 2 3 4 5 6 7 8 9 10
❖
First Edition

For my forget-me-not parents, John and Marie

—D.E.

Love always to T. A. and U.

—J.o.S.

Once upon a time

there was a forgetful porpoise named Seamore.
Seamore lived deep in the deep blue sea.

Like most porpoises, Seamore was kind
and playful.
   In fact, he was probably the sweetest
porpoise you could ever hope to meet.

But unlike most porpoises, Seamore
was very, *very* forgetful.

He forgot *everything*.

He forgot to listen in class.

He forgot who his friends were.

He forgot plans
they'd made together.

And sometimes Seamore
even forgot how to play
his favorite games.

This is what it looked like when
Seamore tried to remember something.

Seamore tried every trick he could think of to fix his memory.

He wrote himself notes but then forgot where he put them.

He tied string around his fins to remind himself of things, but he could never remember which string meant what.

No matter how hard he tried, things only got worse.

Seamore decided he needed more than tricks and gimmicks to solve his problem. If his memory wouldn't come back to him, he was just going to have to go out and find it.

So he swam off alone to do just that.

Beyond the reef, past the old sunken ship, and through the kelp forest Seamore swam. Still his memory was nowhere to be found.

Finally, when he was far, far from home, Seamore saw another porpoise.

"Maybe *he's* seen my memory," Seamore thought.

"Hello there!" he said happily. Seamore swam in closer, then realized he was talking to his own reflection.

Seamore studied himself. He looked just like any other porpoise, as far as he could remember. But then he noticed something peculiar.

"Aha! No wonder I'm forgetful!" he said. "My memory must be slipping right through that hole in my head!"

Seamore couldn't wait to get home
and share his news. But when he did, the
other porpoises only laughed. "Seamore,"
they said, "we *all* have holes in the tops
of our heads! Don't tell us you forgot!"

Seamore smiled sheepishly and slipped
back into the blue.

Moving sadly along and
forgetting to watch
where he was going,
Seamore swam

SMACK!

into a creature he'd
never met before.
It looked a little like a
porpoise, only much,
much bigger. It was
black and white and had
an enormous smile, with
lots of big, sharp teeth.

"Oh, hello. My name is . . . umm, Seamore," Seamore said shyly.

"Hello, Umm Seamore," answered the giant porpoise.

Seamore smiled. "What's your name?" he asked.

"I'll tell you," said the creature, "but first you'll have to count to seven."

Seamore didn't know if he could remember how to count that high, but he tried anyway. "One." This was already hard. "After one is . . . two. Then three. Four. Five. Six . . ."

"KEVIN!" exclaimed the gigantic porpoise. "What are you doing out here on your own?" Kevin asked.

"I can't remember," said Seamore, and he really couldn't.

"Hmm. That's all right. I forget things sometimes, too."

"You do?" asked Seamore, very excited to meet a like-minded mammal.

"Of course I do. Everyone forgets from time to time."

"Not me," confessed Seamore. "I forget *all* the time."

"I bet you could remember some of your favorite things to do," said Kevin.

"Sure," answered Seamore, "that's easy. Come on, I'll show you."

And together they began to play.

They leaped high out of the water.

They blew great big bubbles and watched them
go POP! when they reached the surface.

They dove down deep and swam along the
ocean floor to feel the sand tickle their bellies.

Soon the sun was low in the sky, and it was time to go. But before he swam home, Seamore invited Kevin over for dinner and gave him directions to his house.

"You go straight through the kelp forest and take a left at the sunken ship. I live just past the coral reef."

Seamore rushed to tell the others all about his new friend. He tried his hardest to remember everything about Kevin, and to his amazement, he did!

"He's *how* big?" one porpoise asked.

"And he's *what* color?" said another.

"And he has *how* many teeth?" a third chimed in.

"He's not a giant porpoise! He's a killer whale!" said a fourth.

Just
then a large
shadow spread
over the seafloor.
Everyone scattered
and hid in the reef.
Everyone except
Seamore.

"Am I early? Where is everybody?" Kevin asked.

"They're hiding," Seamore confessed.
"Oh, hide-and-seek! My favorite!"
exclaimed Kevin.

And with that, Kevin began to find the petrified porpoises one by one . . . but he didn't try to scare, or eat, or even bite them. "Gotcha!" he laughed.

When the others saw that Kevin was friendly, they joined in on the game.

It was always
easy to find Kevin,
because he was as
big as a whale.

Later that night everyone sat down to dinner, and Kevin ate only what was on his plate. Seamore's recollection of their day, along with Kevin's impressive coin collection, made the other porpoises forget they had ever been afraid at all. They laughed and told stories, and the seven of them ate until nine.

As for Seamore, he remained as forgetful as ever. Well, *almost*. But now he had Kevin to remind him of the important things.

the End